THE LEGEND OF THE CROSS

WRITTEN BY CHRISSI HART

ILLUSTRATED BY NIKO CHOCHELI

To Anna and Evie - CH

To the memory of Solomon Kurdiani: a world-renowned scientist, pioneer in the science
of Dendrology (the study of trees) and Botany, one of the founders of the Tbilisi State
University, and the creator of the Georgian School of Dendrology. -NC

LCCN: 2001012345
Hardcover ISBN: 978-1-62395-529-8
Paperback ISBN: 978-1-62395-570-0
Published in the United States by Xist Publishing
www.xistpublishing.com
PO Box 61593 Irvine, CA 92601
First Edition

Three seeds of hope once grew on Adam's grave. They sprouted into saplings that merged into a flame shaped tree with three branches at the top. One branch was cypress, one was pine and the other cedar.

When Adam, the first man, reached the end of his long life, he called for his son Seth. "I want you to go to Paradise and ask the angel at the gate to give you the healing oil of mercy so I can anoint my sick body."

eth willingly made the long journey to Paradise. When he arrived, he prayed and wept at the gate until the Archangel Michael came to him. He was dressed in magnificent armor and his wide dark wings swept up behind him. He held a fiery sword in one hand and radiant light, like lightening, shone on his handsome face.

"My father Adam is dying," Seth said. "Could you spare some oil to soothe his passing?"

he angel felt sorry for Seth and put three seeds from
the Tree of Life into his hand. "Fear not, Son of
Adam. Plant these seeds and trust God! When the
tree bears fruit, the Son of God will come and
bring your father Adam into paradise, back
to the tree of mercy."

After several days, Seth returned home. His father had already died and could not smell the sweet fragrance of the seeds. Seth put the seeds in his father's mouth and the Archangel Michael brought Adam to the Garden, where he had been created and buried him in a purple robe.

The seeds grew into
saplings that merged into a
miraculous triple branched tree.
As time passed, people forgot the
meaning of the tree.
However, the tree grew and blossomed
and the leaves stayed green and never died.

t was taller than all the trees of Lebanon and pointed to heaven.

It survived the great flood when God saved Noah and all the animals on the ark.

9

It watched King David sit under its branches and write his psalms.

After King David died, Solomon became king, and built a temple for the Lord. When it was nearly finished, the builders needed one more beam. They searched high and low but could not find one that was suitable.

ne day a woodcutter came to King
Solomon's garden and spotted the
holy tree. He measured it and asked
for it at once.

King Solomon had no choice but to agree for the holy tree to be cut down. But once cut, this beam was like no other! One minute it was long, the next it was short. It would not fit anywhere. It curled at the edges and refused to be placed in the temple. When King Solomon saw the wood change size he became alarmed. "Perhaps I made a mistake and God has another plan for it!"

"This wood is cursed," Solomon's builders exclaimed. So they used the wood to help build a bridge across the Kedron River. By God's grace, they soon found another tree and finished the temple.

One day, the Queen of Sheba traveled to Jerusalem to find out how wise Solomon was and to test him with questions. With her, she brought gifts of gold, precious stones and spices fit for a king. She was carried in a red and gold throne covered with rubies, pearls and other jewels.

n the way the Queen of Sheba was told the special nature of the bridge that she had to cross. She then had a vision of a man, nailed to a cross, hanging over the earth. A voice said, "The hope of the world will hang on that wood." When she reached the bridge she knelt down, kissed the holy wood, then picked up her skirt and humbly waded across the water of the Kedron.

he Queen met King
Solomon in his palace and
was in awe of everything she saw.
She had come searching
for wisdom and found
something greater
than Solomon.
She found God.

17

he Queen of Sheba's vision prompted her to write to the king when she returned home six months later. "The hope of the world will hang on that wood and it will mean the end of your kingdom," she warned.

18

Solomon's face grew pale and his hands trembled as he read the scroll. "How can I destroy this wood that is so holy?" He removed the wood from the bridge, covered it with silver and precious jewels and placed it at the temple gate to be honored.

Years later when he died, the wood was stripped of its jewels and buried in a deep pit, in the city of Jerusalem. Immediately, the pit welled up and formed a magical pool, known as the pool of Bethesda.

or several years the Archangel Raphael visited the pool at certain seasons. Each time he stirred the water with his staff. Many people were healed of their blindness, lameness and paralysis.

he holy wood stayed at the bottom of the pool and
waited for the hope of the world to come.

Many years later, three Kings from the east came with gifts of gold, frankincense and myrrh. They followed a bright star in the east to a cave in Bethlehem where a baby in swaddling clothes lay in a manger. "My son, Jesus will be the light of the world," Mary said as she gazed lovingly at her baby's face.

The years passed and the Son of God performed many wonders and miracles. But God so loved the world that he sent his only son like a lamb to be sacrificed for our sins.

n the day of Christ's crucifixion and suffering, the wood floated up to the surface of the pool.

"That wood is perfect for a cross," a soldier cried out.

25

Just as the Queen of Sheba had been shown, the hope of the world hung on that cross, as foretold by the prophets of old. The earth trembled and darkness blotted out the sun. In that terrible moment, the sun and moon hid their faces and stars fell from the sky.

Βut on the third day, the day of resurrection, the
sun shone like a brilliant diamond in the sky. God
opened the gates to heaven so everyone could enter and
enjoy a new Paradise with Him forever.

And the cypress, the pine and the cedar rejoiced!
For by Christ's holy cross, the three seeds of hope that once grew
on Adam's grave show each of us the narrow path back to the
garden of Paradise.

"And the glory of Libanus shall come to thee, with the cypress, and pine, and cedar together, to glorify My holy place."
(Isaiah 60:13)

The End.

ABOUT THE LEGEND

The legend of the Cross developed between the 4th and 14th centuries and consists of three distinct themes.

The first was told in the 4th century and became part of Church tradition, as did the second. It tells the story of the finding of the precious and life giving Cross by Saint Helena, mother of Saint Constantine. The second legend describes the recovery of the Cross to Jerusalem by Emperor Heraclius in the 7th century after it was stolen by the Persian ruler Chosroes. The third legend, on which this story is based, developed in the 12th century and relates the origin of the wood of the Cross, or the "holy rood," and merges several prophesies of Christ's Cross in the Old Testament. By the end of the 14th century, the three legends merged into a complete narrative known as the Golden Legend told by Jacobus de Voragine, which inspired monumental paintings in Western Europe.

ABOUT THE AUTHOR

Chrissi Hart was born in Cyprus, grew up in England and now lives in York, Pennsylvania with her husband and two children. She is the author of several children's books including, *Under the Grapevine* and *The Hermit, The Icon and The Emperor*. This book is Chrissi's second collaboration with Niko Chocheli and celebrates the holy Cross in both word and image. Chrissi is also a child psychologist and hosts Readings from Under the Grapevine podcast on Ancient Faith Radio. Learn more about her work by visiting her website, www.chrissihart.com

ABOUT THE ILLUSTRATOR

Niko Chocheli was born in Tbilisi, Georgia, the Orthodox Christian nation that built the Monastery of the Cross in Jerusalem. Growing up surrounded by sacred art and nurtured by his mother Leila's deep faith, Niko's illustrations clearly reflect the profound influence of the art and design of the Georgian Orthodox Church. Niko has illustrated several Orthodox children's books, including *The Book of Jonah*, *The Praises*, and *Christ in the Old Testament* and *The Hermit, the Icon, & the Emperor*. Niko lives with his wife Kristen in Doylestown, Pennsylvania, where he runs the Chocheli School of Fine Arts.

Photo Credit Glenn Race

Made in the USA
San Bernardino, CA
15 February 2016